This igloo book
belongs to:

....

D0416687

igloobooks

Published in 2020
by Igloo Books Ltd
Cottage Farm
Sywell
NN6 0BJ
www.igloobooks.com

Copyright © 2019 Igloo Books Ltd
Igloo Books is an imprint of Bonnier Books UK

All rights reserved. No part of this publication may be
reproduced or transmitted in any form or by any means,
electronic, or mechanical, including photocopying, recording,
or by any information storage and retrieval system,
without permission in writing from the publisher.

0520 001
2 4 6 8 10 9 7 5 3 1
ISBN 978-1-83852-215-5

Written by Caroline Richards
Illustrated by Mike Byrne

Designed by Alice Dainty
Edited by Caroline Richards

Printed and manufactured in China

BEE my Friend

igloobooks

Outside in Poppy's garden, she could hear a funny sound.

A BUZZING, WHIZZING, HUMMING...

... noise was whirring all around.

She saw a flash of stripes and knew it was a bumblebee.

"OH, NO! PLEASE HELP!"

squealed Poppy.

"IT'S GOING TO STING ME!"

Poppy was so scared, she tried to run away and hide.
But she quickly grabbed a jar instead and trapped the bee inside.

With her magnifying glass
she peered inside the jar.
Then a voice said,
"My name's Bernard and
I've travelled very far!"

Bernard's wings were tiny.
He had black and yellow fuzz.
"I used to live with
lots of friends,"
he told her with a buzz.

"My colony all flew away
and now I'm on my own.
I'm trying to find
somewhere safe that
I can call my home."

FoR
SaLE

"We bees all do so much to help. Without us not much grows.
We help to make the food you eat and even help make clothes!"

"We fly pollen between flowers on days when it is sunny,
and work hard in our golden hives to make you tasty honey."

"There are lots of scary things," *he said*, "that threaten what we do. A world without us bees won't be the same for all of you."

Poppy was amazed. She said,
"For someone that's
so small...

... you and your great
bee friends do so
much to help us all!"

Bernard smiled at Poppy,
but he didn't feel his best.
His wings drooped, as he yawned
and said, "I need a nice long rest!"

Then Bernard asked for water because it would make him strong.
"Bees aren't at all scary," Poppy thought. "I was so wrong!"

As soon as he felt better,
Bernard had to go away.
"I have to find my colony,
but I'll be back one day!"

"**Thank you**," Bernard called,
as he flew off into the night.
Right then, Poppy knew she had
to help to put things right.

So Poppy asked her grandad if he'd help her plant some flowers.
They put out water, built a hive and worked outside for hours.

Then, one sunny afternoon, she heard a buzzing sound.
Bernard and his fuzzy friends were flying all around!

"Bernard!" shouted Poppy. She couldn't believe her eyes.
"You DID come back," she whispered.
"What a special surprise."

"Your garden is just perfect for us," he said, with a smile.
And all the bees agreed that they would love to stay a while.

Poppy threw a party so her friends could all learn, too.
"Wow," they said, amazed. "We want to help bees, just like you!"

"Thanks to you," buzzed Bernard,
"now we have a happy end.
Poppy you're the best
and I will always...

... BEE
YOUR
FRIEND!"